Escape Into The FOREST

TINA POTTER
KENNY DIETRICH

Cover and art by WILL GOSSAGE

Edited by SYDNEY SHOEMAKER

DEDICATIONS

From Tina

For Ryan, my calm in the chaos. Also for writers
past, present and future: may we be inspired
by those who came before us and hopefully
those who come after us.

From Kenny

In memory of my friend Jeff.

Stay Blessed.

As a fellow writer and proud Appalachian, I was thrilled when Tina and Kenny approached me about editing the second book in their Survival Ember series, and then even more so when they extended the honor by asking me to write the foreword for 'Escape into the Forest'. After my attending Greenup County High School with Tina, I left Eastern Kentucky to acquire separate degrees in Creative Writing and Linguistics from the University of Kentucky. I then went on to leave Kentucky as a whole to pursue screenwriting in Los Angeles, whereupon arriving I completed my first personal screenwriting project as an homage to Appalachian culture and language. Needless to say, the content of this series excited me as much as the job itself.

Tina and Kenny took with this series a profoundly unique approach to the advice that, at some point, every writer has been given:

Write what you know. Because of this, they have managed to expertly represent both Tina's mastery of herbalism, Kenny's vast knowledge of bush-craft survival, and a mutually genuine appreciation for Eastern Kentucky and the Appalachian region, each while simultaneously exhibiting a natural gift for fictional storytelling. Additionally, from their collective ability to embrace the two distinct, yet cohesive voices of John and Ember, they have also been able to illustrate a deeply spiritual connection to nature – one I truly believe exists inherently within every human soul – as it binds a touching, kindred relationship between a father and daughter. As a reader and fellow writer, I so admire their shared, cohesive abilities, not only to tell a compelling story, but to reach into the depths of these characters' hearts and souls to give them each a voice that accurately depicts both the strength and the vulnerability of the Appalachian people.

Though I spent my entire life until age eighteen in Greenup County, it wasn't until I'd already left that I truly began to nurture a genuine appreciation for the region, its culture, and the seemingly boundless extent of talent and art that consistently stems from the people of Eastern Kentucky. Growing up, I thought I resented my living in a small town. It's art like this series, culturally rich and spiritually connected to the roots of Appalachia, that reminds me of the true nature of my alleged resentment and prompts further promise to myself to never again take my home for granted.

On top of all that soul-wrenching earnestness, because I didn't start working with the series until its second installment, I also got to approach this job as a fan. I couldn't wait to find out how Ember and John would take on the secrets in the forest, to learn from the exhibitions of their various skills, and to be inevitably inspired by the will of these two characters to always do the right thing. It's my honor and privilege to present you with this, the second book of the Survival Ember series: 'Escape into the Forest'.

CHAPTERS

VII

"survivalism noun
sur·viv·al·ism | \ sər-ˈvī-və-ˌli-zəm \
Definition of survivalism:
an attitude, policy, or practice based on
the primacy of survival as a value"

Survivalism. (n.d.) In Merriam-Webster's dictionary.
Retrieved from https://www.merriam-webster.com/
dictionary/survivalism

BOOK TWO

CHAPTER ONE

~Ember~

It was silent. I remember that.

The sky was clear, not a single cloud for as far as my eyes could see. The sun bathed me in warm rays as I laid in the grassy field. The silence was absolute - not even a bird's call dared to break it. It wasn't heavy, though, that silence. Even now, as I recall it, I don't really pay it much mind. It felt normal...for that place, anyways.

The air was still and light.

How can I describe it? It was as if there was some change to the pressure in the air, or something different altogether. When I looked around and slowly pulled myself up off the ground, I felt myself all but float into standing position, as if gravity no longer existed. It made me think that the nature of my movements had changed, like they'd somehow been heavier before.

The field itself was large. I turned and saw that one side of it stretched out forever into the horizon. I looked to the other side of me and saw a dense line of trees. Could it have been the edge of a forest? It seemed like it.

I know it wasn't anywhere I had been before. The endless field was welcoming. I felt like I should lie back down and just...*remain*. I felt like there was no time, no reason to go anywhere else. Even if there had been anywhere else to go, there wasn't any need.

I almost didn't look back at those trees. I almost stayed in that place, one void of the burden of memory. I had a name; I came from somewhere. And, while it felt like time didn't matter - or maybe didn't even exist - I knew that I had spent it somewhere else before. A need to get back to that lost, unknown place began to grow in the back of my mind.

But the forest still waited. I remember thinking that maybe the answer was in there - the answer to something important.

I couldn't fight it any longer. With my new fluidity of motion, I ran to the tree line. Once again, my movements were easy, light, and smooth. There was an absence of underbrush. If a forest could ever have had a meticulous groundskeeper, this one did. My view reached far into the forest, and I walked into it without fear of tripping over any type of natural debris like logs or rocks. No, this forest was absent of logs. The trees were tall, maybe hundreds of feet, and healthy. They lined up one after another, evenly spaced in each direction. There weren't any signs of bushes; there weren't any signs of animals. It was just me and the trees.

So, I continued to run. Raising my knees with each stride and picking up speed, I tried to remember. My struggle to recall where I was going, where I had come from - it seemed to be the only struggle of this place. The trees still watched; they still stood. The sun still shone. I was the only thing in motion, the only change in the peaceful monotony.

Then I came across a break in the trees. Even there, in the clearing, I felt the invisible eyes of the trees that lined the edge of the circle. They still watched; they still stood. The sun still shone. But now there was something else, an object lying on the grass under the sun, just as I had been. Walking closer to the object, I realized it was a pack. I bent down next to it, and, while picking up the dirty thing, I remember thinking how it didn't belong in this place. In a place as perfect as this, the backpack was too imperfect. Maybe that's why I felt like I belonged somewhere else too.

I found the zipper to the main pocket, but it wouldn't budge; I couldn't open the pack. I slipped the straps of the pack onto my shoulders anyway, and started running forward, back into the trees. But something was different now. For the first time, I felt some weight to my movement. As I endured on, I once more tried to remember where I had been before all this, where I was trying to go.

Slowly, the pack also began to grow heavier. I started to feel like time had begun to tick once more, and that gravity was slowly coming back. I suddenly realized that I, myself, had become a part of the vast silence, but when I tried to speak, no noise came from my mouth.

Even now, as I recall that run through the eerie, wooded perfection, the same questions race through my mind: *What was happening? Where was I going? Why was I there?*

I tried to shout as I continued to run through that seemingly never-ending stretch. Then came another break in the forest, and this time, the only difference was a mound that rose up from the center, completely covered in newly grown grass. It, too, was perfect and undisturbed.

Only, I knew something about it wasn't natural…*wasn't perfect.*

My pack slipped off and fell to the ground behind me. I turned around and noticed the zipper I had struggled with before was now gone, as if it'd been completely removed. The pack was open. Reaching inside, I finally felt something opposite of the warmth that was surrounding me in that place: cold, hard metal. I clutched my fingers around the cold, hard, metal thing, and when I pulled my hand from the pack, out with it came a small shovel. I turned back around and fell to my knees, watching my hand adjust its grip and aim the shovel overtop of the mound.

I plunged the spade's tip deep into the grass, and, all at once, a sharp clash of thunder rang out and broke the silence just as I broke ground. The shovel fell and my hands went straight to my ears; everything had become too loud at the same exact time. Birds screeched out into the air, but it sounded to my ears more like the hard screeching of metal-on-metal.

I remember wanting to give up but knowing that I couldn't. I picked up the shovel and stabbed it into the ground once more. Thunder clashed again as a bolt of lightning struck the mound. I jumped and moved back quickly while the sky grew darker. Wind came from all directions, and my head was filled with a sharp, agonizing pain. As I lifted my head toward the sky, and the massive gusts of air swirling around me pulled mercilessly through my hair, I finally heard my own voice calling out in the wind. And I suddenly realized what I had been shouting all along: *"Dad!"*

* * *

My eyes were sensitive as they opened to an onslaught of fluorescent lighting. I could hear monitors keeping status, a phone ringing, and people talking out in the hall. Dad's head rested at the end of the bed, as if he had passed out while praying. I looked over next to me and saw Mom, audibly praying while sitting next to Tanner. His arm was in a sling and his eyes were pointed down toward the floor. I tried to speak, but my head was hurting too bad. Instead, I moved my leg closest to Dad.

Startled by the motion, Dad's head shot up and he met my eyes. I wanted to close my eyes again; my head hurt so bad, but I also wanted to stay awake and talk to Dad. I felt like there was something important to tell him. I couldn't remember, though.

"Hey, Em, stay awake sweetheart," Dad said softly. He stroked my hand, comforting me in my new lucid state, then looked urgently over his shoulder and called out to the open door of my hospital room. *"Can I get a nurse in here?"*

After the nurse saw that I was awake, she had the doctor come in to explain that I had a mild concussion and told me what I needed to do to help the healing process. It was hard to pay attention because, as he spoke, I suddenly noticed that the hospital air felt cold on my skin, and that my arms were covered in small, raised bumps.

Somewhere in the doctor's spiel, I found out why Tanner was so bandaged up. Apparently, he'd walked away with a broken arm and a bit of whiplash - I reckon we both managed to leave the crash in a lot better shape than we could have. After what couldn't have been more than three or so minutes, the doctor left, and I was once again alone with my family.

My eyes moved over to Mom, whom I realized had been crying, and she grabbed my hand.

"Are you hungry, honey? Do you want me to get you something to drink?"

I closed my eyes. It hurt to talk.

"Maybe some water, please."

The cold water ran down my throat and saturated my dry, cracked lips. The glare of the hospital lights was almost too much, and I squinted. I felt like I could sense the humming of the electric radiating through them.

"Can someone turn the lights off?" I mumbled. "I just want to sleep."

Mom walked over to the switch by the door and killed the fluorescent ceiling fixtures one-by-one, until the only light in the room came from a small crack between the curtains.

As the dimness washed over, I felt the muscles in my face relax. I opened my eyes and turned back to Tanner.

"How're you feeling, bro?"

He shrugged. "I-I'm glad you're okay, Em. I-I'll b-be back, I'm going to l-look for another bathroom."

And with that, my brother got up from his chair and walked out.

"He feels guilty." Dad was rubbing the back of his neck, rolling his head back and forth.

"It wasn't his fault..."

At least, I didn't think it was.

I couldn't remember.

"He said that he wasn't paying full attention to the road, Em."

Wasn't he?

We were somewhere near the forest heading back to the house - I remembered that much.

Dad sat forward in his chair and met my eyes as he spoke softly to me.

"That you guys are safe now and weren't injured worse than you are, that's all that matters. You guys seemed too frantic on the phone, though. You were panicked, Em. What happened? What did you have to show me?"

I thought about it for a moment. I couldn't remember what I had told him.

My phone, where was it?

"What did you see, sweetheart?"

My hand started shaking in Mom's as a chill ran up my spine. I couldn't remember anything but the trees of the forest, standing tall above my head as I had looked up into the rain.

What was I doing out there?

"My head hurts, Dad."

Dad sat back down in his chair. "I know, Em. Just rest, okay? Don't worry about it now. We can talk about it later."

Tanner didn't come back anytime soon. If he did, he must've been outside my room.

CHAPTER TWO

Now that the dramatic event was a week behind us and both my kids were home safe and sound, I finally got a decent night's sleep. I opened my eyes to see the light as it came through the part in the curtains. I must have slept later than I usually did, but I still woke up before my alarm went off - *beep, beep, beep* - but not by much. I turned it off and climbed out of bed while Maria continued to sleep.

Tanner was released a couple of days after the car accident, however Ember ended up staying a little longer due to the concussion. The only major injury was Tanner's broken arm (thank the good Lord), but it sure scared Maria and me. I felt better that morning, having slept for the first time in days. After Ember recounted the events leading up to the accident - at least what she could remember - I wanted to find out more. I wanted to at least look for the missing cell phone too. I hoped once I talked with the fellas about what they uncovered I would have more answers.

The phone buzzed again.

'I thought I turned the alarm off, ' I whispered to myself.

I quickly grabbed it and realized it wasn't the alarm on my phone, but rather a call coming in, with Robert's name heading the screen. I answered quietly so as to not wake Maria, and then quickly made my way to the kitchen.

"Hello."

"Hey, John, this is Robert."

'Yes, Robert, I know. I have caller-ID, and I can see your name on my phone,' I thought to myself.

"Hey, buddy. What's up?" Robert did this with every phone call, so it had become our normal routine. I guess he thought people couldn't tell who was calling - *bless his heart.*

"I need you to come to the diner for breakfast this morning. Jeff and I will be waiting on you."

"Okay, I'll grab a shower and be on my way."

We hung up and I headed to the bathroom. Fifteen minutes later I was clean, dressed, and out the door - all before anyone else in the house was awake. I led my old pick-up, Nelly, to the diner and saw Robert and Jeff, already seated in the nearly empty restaurant. The breakfast crowd hadn't arrived yet, but it was still very early.

The bell above the door chimed as I entered, and my heart went to my throat when both of my buddies looked up to greet me. Jeff's forehead was all bandaged up, and one of Robert's eyes had been blackened something awful. I pulled up a chair and slowly took my seat, then drummed up the calmest and most cautious voice I could manage.

"What happened?" I asked.

So, Jeff began to recount the events leading up to their state.

"We found Niki's address through a friend who rents her a house close to the Federal forest, and we went to take a look."

Niki. Even just hearing the name of the cagey woman from the forest always made me uneasy to my stomach. But hearing it now, judging by the looks of my friends, I let all the doubt I'd had about that uneasiness before fly out the window.

"Robert faked a flower delivery, and I rode shotgun to be the lookout. No one was home when we pulled up to the house, so Robert motioned for me to join him on the porch. We decided to peek in the windows

17

and take a look around - that's when we noticed a bunch of backpacks laying on the living room floor. You're right, John! Something is going on!"

Jeff went on enthusiastically. "Suddenly we heard her voice from behind us. We turned around and saw Niki standing there - *I kid you not* - wielding a bloody knife! We took off running for the delivery van. Robert was a few steps ahead of me, dropped his flowers, and when he turned around to pick them up...*WHAM!* I ran into him! We collided head-to-head, thus the black eye on the big guy and the cut on me." He gently touched the bandage on his forehead, then continued, "We made it back to the van and drove away."

I sat quiet for a moment, soaking it all in, and looked at both of my buddies (more like brothers, really) as they examined their battle scars. They looked back at me with serious expressions, anxiously waiting on my response to break the silence.

"Bwahaha!" I laughed out loud suddenly and uncontrollably, unable to stop.

Jeff folded his arms and leaned back in his chair.

Robert had the look of a hurt puppy, and his broad torso covered the table as he came in closer to whisper. *"It's not funny, John! This could be serious."*

"I know, brother. I know." I gained control of myself and stopped the guffaw. "But if you could just see yourselves."

Jeff leaned in beside Robert. "Believe me, we know how we look - our wives keep reminding us. But all joking aside, I think this is serious."

I managed to maintain a straight face. "I agree. I'm sorry for laughing, especially since I'm the one who got you into this mess."

They both sat back in their chairs.

"So, where do we go from here?" Jeff asked.

"I think it's safe to say it's worth further investigating," I added. "I believe it's time we get Dave involved. Or at least let him take a look into things."

As if on cue, our friend Dave the Sheriff walked in, removed his hat, and looked around. He spotted us and headed over to our table.

"What's up, fellas?"

Instead of responding, Robert and Jeff hid their injuries the best they could, and I tried to suppress another laugh as Dave slowly pulled up a chair. Like Robert, Dave was a big guy: tall, broad shouldered, and what we called 'country strong'. The four of us took up a lot of space and made the old diner four-top look like a children's table.

After we all readjusted ourselves, Dave looked at me out of the corner of his eye, and then over at the other two. I had a seriously stupid smile on my face because I was about ready to burst.

After a long moment of staring at them, he looked back my way. "What's going on?"

Somehow keeping a straight face, I started telling the story all the way from the beginning. Robert and Jeff joined in eagerly during their parts, both unveiling their hands to display the extent of their wounds. As I recounted the past events, my mood changed, and it became more obvious to me and everyone at the table just how big a deal this really was.

Dave leaned way back in his chair with his arms folded, frowning so hard that someone who didn't know him any better may presume his face was permanently stuck that way. The two hind legs of the chair protested under his bulk with a creak. He started with shaking his head, and I knew it wasn't going to be good.

"*What...were...you...thinking?*" He spat out each word one-at-a-time, then let the weight of the demand hang in the air while he slowly brought his chair back to all fours.

"You guys need to back off. This is *not* the way things are done!" By the time he got out the last word, he may as well have been yelling.

I looked around - luckily the place was still empty - then tried to respond, "But look here-"

"No, *you* look here!" Dave cut me off. "This is nuts and probably your all's crazy imaginations. Does this have anything to do with Ember's car wreck?"

Everyone remained quiet.

He shook his head again. "I can't believe you guys. It stops now!"

We all sat quietly, looking down at the table as Dave gave us each our own special, individual look of disgust. He unfolded his arms, and then there was a long, heavy pause.

"I will look into it. *Properly.*" He let that set in for a minute, allowing us to understand that, although he thought it was crazy talk, he still would honor his friends' request.

"Now, which one of you knuckleheads are buying me breakfast?" And with that, he waved the waitress over to take our orders.

Chapter Three

~Ember~

I walked through the hallway of the school, all too aware of the way I must've looked to the other students. I was bruised where the airbag hit me, and I knew I looked like I hadn't slept in days.

In the nights since I'd returned home from the hospital, the ability to sleep at all had become my nightly feat, and the same restless dream had woken me each morning since the wreck.

The dream goes like this:

I'm standing in the forest. The trees are towered over me, stretching as high up into the sky as I can see.

I try to move forward, but my feet feel heavy and my movements are sluggish and clumsy. I look down at my uncooperative feet and realize that I'm standing in a deep expanse of mud. I begin to sink, slowly at first, deeper into the thick, sinister molasses. I start to panic, now, as the earth pulls harder and I sink faster, faster. I fall forward and reach toward the area of hard ground in front of me, but as my desperate hand falls upon the grass, it melts away into the mud. I claw and claw at the edge, and each time, over and over, it melts away to become part of the mud that's consuming me. I'm in over my shoulders now. Even if there were hard land to reach for that had yet to melt away, I'm no longer able to lift my covered arms. I'm struggling, hyperventilating, when suddenly, something raises out of the mud in front of me. But there's mud in my eyes and it's too dark to see...

And then I wake in a puddle of sweat and panic.

Mom tried to get me to stay home again this morning. She said I needed more time to recuperate from whatever trauma I seem to have experienced prior to the wreck. After Dad's account of the phone call, Tanner's silence on the matter, and my amnesia of the event, she didn't want to let me out of her sight.

"Hey, Ember..." My best friend, Chelsea, reached out for my arm and pulled me out of my thoughts.

"Oh, hey, Chels."

"Em, you had me worried when I heard about the wreck!"

"It wasn't anything serious. I came out of the hospital practically the same day."

Well, that was sort of true.

I pulled my english book out of my locker and closed the door behind it. Chelsea was eyeing me closely and fell into step beside me as I started towards class.

"Something's different. You don't seem alright for something not so serious."

"I've been having a weird recurring dream is all. Well, that and I do have some lingering effects of the concussion."

Chelsea's eyes widened at the mention of the dream. She was a firm believer in the clairvoyant nature of dreams, always able to make some meaningful interpretation or another out of them. Then she'd go on to justify the significance of it all with stories about prophetic dreams of the past, like Joseph's in the Bible.

"You have to tell me! What's this dream? What are you wearing in the dream? Do you see fish in it? How many?"

"Woah, slow down... There aren't any fish."

We turned the corner of the hall and walked straight to the classroom where our classmates were already flooding in to claim their seats. Chelsea stayed right on my heels and sat down next to me.

I tried to keep my face down. I didn't feel like talking about the wreck with anyone else, but the other students were already staring. A girl named Jada came over, anyways, wearing a bright red shirt. The intensity of the color triggered a sharp pain in my head.

"Hey, Ember, it stinks what happened. If you need anything let me know, okay?"

"Thanks, Jada."

She walked away and Chelsea rolled her eyes.

"She was just being nice, Chels..."

"That's fine, even though she never gave us the time of day before. But" - she leaned in close and finished with a whisper - *"you need to tell me about this dream!"*

Just then, Mr. Cravitts cleared his throat and started calling attendance.

I quickly wrote 'talk in the library after class' on a piece of loose paper and passed it to Chelsea. She rolled her eyes again.

She's the queen of sass today.

The now looming conversation about the dream did nothing to help me with the already impossible task of paying attention to Mr. Cravitts' lecture. It wasn't just English, though. It was every class. In fact, this wasn't anything new anymore. I'd been having issues focusing ever since the day I saw that woman burying something in the forest. A feeling deep down inside me kept drawing me back to that moment, however, what happened there, I still couldn't remember.

After class, Chelsea practically dragged me by the hand all the way to the library. There wasn't any consideration for my physical state - she was a girl on a mission. The grey light coming through the tall floor-to-ceiling windows spilled over us as we made our way to my favorite spot in the back corner. It was still foggy out, but there was the promise of sunshine later in the day. The dusky library was practically empty this early in the morning, but if we stayed tucked away in the back, there was a good chance we would go unnoticed.

Keeping her voice low, Chelsea dove straight into the topic at hand. "So, spill it, tell me everything. There's got to be a reason this dream keeps occurring every night."

So I went into detail about the dream that I had earlier that morning and every morning since coming home those past few days. She paid close attention, hanging onto my every word. Aside from the occasional nodding of her head, she didn't speak until I was totally finished.

"Do you recognize anything from this dream? Where you are? Or what you feel?"

I leaned back and stared up at the ceiling, letting the memory of the dream float back up to the surface of my mind as if it, too, was floating. I pictured it and all the memories surrounding it leaving my body and hovering away, all the way up to the high, vaulted ceiling. But suddenly the sound of thunder rumbled deep and low, pulling me from my daze.

Maybe it was getting ready to storm. Maybe the weatherman was wrong about sunshine today.

The thunder rumbled again, louder this time, but I still tried to focus on the dream. Nothing was coming to mind as familiar, other than the feeling of drowning.

"Chelsea…"

"Yes?"

Then it hit me: *the mud.* In the dream, I'm sinking in the mud. But in reality - in some lost memory of what *actually happened* - I think I'd been digging in it.

If only I could remember what was coming up out of it at the end of my dream, maybe that would answer what I saw.

"I think I saw something in the forest. Actually, I know I did. Because whatever happened in the forest before the wreck, it was why we were leaving so fast."

Tanner had to know. Why hadn't he told me yet? I needed to go talk to him. Why wasn't he speaking up?

The sudden clamor of books falling off one of the shelves made Chelsea and me both jump in our seats. A boy with a nervous grin came out from behind his hiding spot and started picking up the spilled books on the floor.

"I'm so sorry, girls. I was just trying to waste some time looking at titles."

He looked up at us and gave a sideways toss of his head to get his goofy brown hair out of his eyes. Chelsea shot me a raised eyebrow, and I knew she and I both recognized him immediately as the cute boy that just started attending our church with Mamaw Dawson, the one whose mom had died.

"It's okay. What're you looking for?" she asked.

He stood up and placed the stack of poetry books on the shelf.

"Just a way to escape class for a minute. I'm not actually a big poetry kind of guy, believe it or not. What are you guys doing?"

The question seemed to be directed at both of us, but his eyes were locked with mine. I hurriedly looked down for something else to focus on, but there was clearly no book in front of me to use as an excuse. *Real smooth, Em.*

"We're supposed to be in study hall," I mumbled.

"Oh, cool. Hey, haven't I seen you at church?"

At this point, my annoying best friend was practically dancing in her seat. I raised both of my eyebrows at her and she got the hint.

"I'm just gonna go ahead and go but I'll see ya later, Em!" And with that, Chelsea grabbed her stuff and practically skipped out of the library.

That wasn't what I was hinting at!

And then, as if I wasn't already feeling awkward enough just being alone with him, the cute, goofy-haired boy walked over and sat down, right next to me in Chelsea's empty spot.

"My name's Dan. I just recently moved here from Columbus."

"Cool. I'm Ember."

He leaned close and spoke low.

"So, what's there to do around here? All I see are trees and dollar stores."

"Well, sometimes the local kids go out cow tipping when they get bored."

He smirked. "That could be interesting."

"Yeah, and if things get really desperate, they'll go snipe hunting."

He sat back in the chair and let out a chuckle.

"Oh yeah, that seems about right!"

Clearly, he'd already heard it all before.

"Okay, well, are you into anything outdoorsy anyways?"

"I never spent any time in any woods and I'm not one for sports really. I did climb at a rock-climbing gym near where I lived."

Well, that's something interesting.

"I've never been rock climbing before. We do have a lot of cliffs near us, though. I'm not sure I'd be good at it."

"Like I said, I've never done much outside. I've only ever climbed indoors."

"How long have you been climbing?"

"Ever since I was ten. Mom and Dad would be busy with work, so they bought me a membership for after school. I ended up liking it better than home most days, so that's where I stayed."

That hit me hard. Chelsea had told me at church that she had heard that both his mom and dad had passed away and now he was living with his grandmother. I couldn't imagine what he was going through.

Now what was I supposed to say?

"Well, you must be great at it by now if you've been climbing that long. How old are you?"

"I'm seventeen. So, seven years climbing, I guess."

So, he's a year older than me.

Just then, we heard a door shut in the front of the room. We both leaned back to see that Mr. Frank, the janitor, had walked into the library - *Dan was safe for now.* As we sat back up, I returned my attention to carefully watching Dan.

I was trying to study him, trying to read his face. It held a tight smile, but his eyes were tired. I couldn't help but think how emotionally drained he must've been.

"How long has it been since you climbed?" I asked.

"It's been almost six months now."

"Why did you stop? Was it because there's no climbing gyms here or...?"

"I don't know... Maybe I'll tell you sometime later. I should get back to class."

I must've asked too much.

I felt my face go beet red as I watched him hurry from the room. He flashed me a little wave on the way out the door, and the butterflies that were already in my stomach went into a full-on frenzy.

I clumsily gathered my things and then got up to leave as well, resolving to find wherever Chelsea had run off to. But, upon heading to the door, I was stopped by Mr. Frank.

"Hey, girl. What's up? You look a little tired."

Usually, Mr. Frank and I talked for a bit about the recent things I'd been into. I had told him everything from my joining Dad on his jobs in the woods to my goals for the future.

Maybe he could help me understand my recurring dream.

"I've not been sleeping well, actually."

Mr. Frank stopped pushing his cart and crossed his arms as he leaned against the wall.

"Well, now, why is that?"

"I've been having a weird dream. I went with my brother - a little over a week ago - out to the forest, and something happened that made me rush back. We wrecked, though, and now I can't remember what I found. My dream has been repeating ever since, where I find myself in the mud when- "

At that moment, the bell rang. As a bunch of kids flooded the hallway on their way to the next class, I noticed that my janitor friend had moved from his relaxed stance and was now standing straight up.

"What drew you out to the forest originally?" Mr. Frank's thick Brooklyn accent slipped through as he looked at me over his gold-framed, '70s-style glasses.

I thought carefully. "I saw something out there at one point that made me return to investigate, but I can't remember what I ended up finding."

A teacher down the hall was hollering for the students who were loitering by the lockers to get to their next class, and I knew my time was cut short.

"What part of the forest were you in? Do you think you can let me know if you remember what it is you saw?"

"Sure, I'll try."

I started off but he grabbed the strap of my bag.

"Do your best to let me know if you do, in fact, remember anything, okay?"

"Okay."

His eyes were steely and serious.

"I really mean it. I'm curious, myself."

As I pulled my bag out of his grasp and rushed off to class, my blood ran cold at the way Mr. Frank had been acting. I was suddenly even more concerned than I'd been before - *I didn't even think that was possible.*

C HAPTER F OUR

~John~

I felt better after confessing to Dave and letting him take over the investigation. I reckon I should have done that from the start, because it sure was a weight lifted from my shoulders.

After breakfast at the diner, my day was going great. I started a small kitchen remodel and ended up working a little later than usual. No matter, I got a lot accomplished and was proud of the day's work.

Feeling positive for the first time in a while, I loaded up Nelly and headed towards the house. It was starting to get dark a lot earlier, and the sun had just begun to go down, filling the sky with pastel colors. My favorite song came on the Christian radio station, and I felt like it was the end of a perfect day.

I whipped up the gravel driveway and had to brake quickly to avoid hitting a visiting vehicle.

"Whoa, that was close," I thought aloud. "Wonder who's visiting for supper."

I grabbed my lunch box out of the truck's cab and headed towards the front porch, whistling the song I had just heard.

I stopped mid-stride. *"No way…"*

It took all but a second for my brain to register that the vehicle in the driveway belonged to the woman from the woods, and as soon as it did, I took off in a dead sprint toward the house. I came flying through the front door like a madman, not knowing what to expect. The adrenaline was rushing through my body like the flu.

Like it was perfectly normal, Maria and Niki were sitting at the kitchen table, sipping on cups of tea. I was so taken aback that I almost dropped my lunch box.

This can't be happening.

The shock must have been written all over my face, because they both looked at me like I had horns growing from my forehead.

I decided to speak up first. "Well, what a surprise. I'm beginning to see you all over the place."

"Like I said, I'm new to this town and I needed to meet some people. What better place to start than here?" Niki said. She paused to let it sink in. "Besides, you and Maria are known as good people who are involved in the community, and that's who I need as friends."

The sound of her saying my wife's name sent chills down my spine.

How did she find out where we live? I guess it's really not a secret, but what else has she learned? How deep has she been digging?

"John, I'll be leaving so I don't interrupt your family time," Niki said, standing from the table. "Ember and Tanner will be home soon, and I'm sure Maria is planning a tasty dinner."

I could feel the blood rush to my face and neck as she talked about my kids...*my family.*

I shot Maria a glance, but she showed no change in expression. Her elusive gaze stayed locked onto Niki. "You're more than welcome to stay for supper."

"I appreciate it, but I must be going. It was very nice meeting you, and thank you for the hospitality," Niki responded.

Maria stood up and they both pushed their chairs under the table. She extended a hand to Niki. "It's been great meeting you, and I hope I get to know you better."

Oh, she's sparring now.

As she headed to the front door, Niki stopped shoulder-to-shoulder beside me, then looked straight at me with her piercing blue eyes.

"I look forward to getting to know you guys as well," she said.

She put one of her arms around my back and used the other arm to grab my hand in hers, then squeezed until I felt her nails start to dig into mine.

Maria could see what was going on - truthfully, she'd dug in just hard enough for me to almost question the message. But I knew what she was doing.

I could feel that my face had turned another shade of red, and sweat had started to bead-up on my brow. This was clearly part of her plan - to throw me off guard - and she had succeeded. Niki had left me speechless.

I heard the front door close quietly but didn't hear her clear the porch.

As I stood in the same spot, with my head down looking for fingernail marks in my palm, Maria walked up beside me. She folded her arms across her chest and stood silently, watching Niki drive away. I still couldn't tell what she was thinking until she broke the silence.

"She's dangerous, John, and I don't like her."

I slowly turned around to look at the door where Maria was still staring, not sure what I was going to see. After the shock I'd received coming home, nothing would surprise me.

"I don't think she is who she says she is," Maria said. "There wasn't any dirt under her nails. And did you catch the slightest hint of an accent? I don't mean the country dialect we have - I mean from a country outside of the U.S. There was so much more I noticed but, the bottom line is, something's fishy with little Miss Niki."

My wife has always been an excellent judge of character and very observant. There's never been anyone else whose opinion I've respected more. On top of her being a great listener and slow to judge, I've never seen her misinterpret a person's motive.

"John, you need to take care of this before someone gets hurt."

Enough second guessing myself. Something needs to be done with the lady from the forest.

CHAPTER FIVE

I gave Maria strict instruction to keep our place on lockdown. We've had this drill many times, so she knew what that meant. But this time it wasn't a drill.

We took extra precautions to secure our house and property without looking like we were getting ready for the apocalypse. For instance, we closed and locked the driveway gate at night, made sure all the outside lights were on (including the ones on the outbuildings), and left nothing outside that hadn't been nailed down or could be locked. We also drew all the blinds and curtains - day and night - and kept the exterior doors locked at all times. Of course, we continued our normal routines as well, like using deadbolt locks, window locks, and keeping the cameras on the front and back doors. Most of all, we trusted *no one*! Not delivery guys, not people knocking at the door, not anyone that wasn't known to be a friend.

I hated to leave the house, but I had a Trader's Meeting to go to and, in light of recent events, I wanted to go. I hopped into Nelly, moved the gear shift on the steering column to reverse, got her turned around, and headed down the road. The truck bounced along while the evening sun hung heavy in the sky, and my surroundings were tinged with a slight orange hue. It was the golden hour.

I turned onto the road to head down Route 23, and as the forest turned into Finley land, all signs of development turned into a sea of absolute nothingness that stretched on for miles.

These pines!

No matter how often I went there, I couldn't get over those majestic trees. Once in every person's life, they come across a tree or group of trees that touch the very fabric of their being. Those pines stood tall with authority. They had been alive for decades-on; they knew the secrets the forest holds, and they reached for the heavens as if reaching for God himself. Those trees knew God, and they praised Him with their strength. "Then shall the trees of the wood sing out at the presence of the LORD, because He cometh to judge the earth." 1 Chronicles 16:33

After a few miles, I turned off the asphalt road and crossed the line of pines onto a hidden drive. Single-lane and unmarked, the old dirt road led deep into the heavily wooded home of the Finleys. A humble folk with a small home, one might not guess at first glance that the Finleys actually own the largest acreage of anyone in town. They were also a founding family - one of the oldest of the town. You sure wouldn't know to look at them.

As I made my way up to the house, I saw Mrs. Finley sitting on her porch steps. We exchanged a nod as I drove past her house and deeper into the property. I stopped at the old metal gate that sat where the farm met the woods. It was being guarded by Marc Finley, the oldest grandson. Although the gate was a little rusty and aged, it was maintained and kept in perfect working order.

Marc recognized Nelly and me right away. He grabbed the latch and raised the metal bar that locked the gate to allow me to pass. I cranked my window down to speak.

"What's up buddy?"

"Hey John, how are ya?" Marc shot me a friendly smile.

"What's going on tonight? Anything exciting?" I asked.

"Man, you should see Patrick's newest tomahawk. It is a beauty." Marc lived for all things forged, and the enthusiasm was clear in his voice.

"Cool, can't wait to see it. He always does amazing work," I replied, showing true enthusiasm of my own. "I better get up there. I don't want to be the last to get set up."

"Nah, you won't be. Mike is always last to show, and he still hasn't passed the gate yet," Marc said, looking past my truck and down the road.

"Alright, brother. See ya later." I prepared to head up the hill to the gathering.

He looked back at me. "Okay, buddy. See ya around."

I drove into the woods, following the two graveled tracks that most people would mistake for a four-wheeler or horse trail. After a while, I came across the clearing where the meeting was to take place. I pulled Nelly into my usual spot parked amongst the vehicular medley of pick-ups, ATV's, side-by-sides, pull-behind carts, and trailers of all shapes and sizes. From the old truck cab, I observed the camp.

Yup, same as ever.

The only thing that had changed about the clearing over the years I'd been invited here, on Old Man Finley's land, was the height of the old oak, fir, beech, and poplar trees that formed the circle around it. Finley never allowed for his land to be timbered, so these towering old trees had been around longer than most others in the area, but he had emptied the forest floor within the clearing of all other brush and undergrowth.

I got out of the cab and looked up at the evening sun's peeking through the wide canopy above. Any minute now it would begin to set, to creep out of view from the clearing and settle in behind the hills in the distance. It was beautiful, and I was glad I'd decided to push through my exhaustion to attend the meeting.

The Traders Community has always been by invitation only, so you wouldn't know about it unless Old Man Finley, himself, had invited you. The meetings were an opportunity for the most skilled tradesmen in town to gather and expend their varying crafts amongst one another. There was always a real sense of honor and pride in ourselves and the community when we all came together.

The camp was abuzz with life. People were talking, laughing, and shouting as they bartered or haggled. The clanging sound of a hammer rang through the evening air as Patrick Kent, our blacksmith, worked on an order from his flatbed trailer that he'd turned into a portable shop.

When I pulled Nelly up to the camp, I was greeted by the smell of a fire and the strips of venison that were roasting overtop of it. As I looked around and took it all in, I was filled with a sense of gratitude that I was there.

It truly is an amazing thing to be a part of. It's like stepping back in time to the way things used to be - the way they *should* be.

No money was accepted there; it was by trade of skill only. You bartered with the other members, offering something you made or did in turn for what you wanted. It was basically the old bartering system. You could find anything and everything there: food, tools, soft goods, knives, guns, animals and master services.

Some of the women in the community would sell their knitted and sewn goods, and one of the women by the name of Eliza Moore would actually spin the wool that Tom Briggs had sheared from his sheep.

The Flanery brothers could fabricate and repair anything metal, and they had the skills to do things with steel and aluminum that you couldn't imagine.

Mike would bring in honey and beeswax. Edna would bring in canned and dry goods. And so on and so forth.

In addition to his being the host and founder of the community, Finley himself was the gunsmith of the community. He had, what you would call, an apprentice, a local young man by the name of Ryan, who was learning his trade at Finley's direction. Ryan's girlfriend, Kinsey, came to the meetings too. She sold candles, pastries and bread, all made by herself.

It was getting dark, and people were starting to light their lanterns while the Flannerys were kindling up more fires in the fire pits. Through the dim light of the fires and the setting sun, I scanned the clearing for Old Man Finley. I found him sitting at a table with Ryan and decided to walk over.

"Hello, Mr. Finley. How are you?" I reached out and shook his hand.

"Oh, fair to midland, John. It's good to see ya. Maria and the kids doing okay?"

"Everyone is doing well. Thanks for asking. How's the knife work going?"

"Not too slow these days. Picking up, actually. Ryan's been taking over some of my orders; I can't do it as much anymore," he said. "Did you bring any furs?"

I nodded, understanding just what he meant, but Finley was getting up there in age and his eyesight wasn't the best anymore, so I went on talking. "Yes, of course, I've actually got some great pelts this evening."

We continued the small talk and discussed the season's crop yields, but just when I was about to mention the lady in the forest, I looked over and realized we were about to be interrupted. Sharon, our local basket weaver, and her husband approached the table, and the conversation took a different direction. I decided I'd wait to bring it up.

More people arrived over the next half hour or so - there were about thirty families in total. Soon a hush fell over the camp as people grabbed their chairs and made their way to the center of the clearing. There was no order of seating. Old Man Finley stood up and addressed the small crowd.

"Hello, everyone. Shall we pray and start the meeting?"

"Aye!" Everyone answered in unison.

"Ryan, care to lead us in prayer?"

Finley sat down and motioned for another young man by the name of Jacob, our local bowyer and a soon-to-be doctor, to stand and lead us all in prayer. As Jacob took off his hat and stood, we all bowed our heads.

"God in Heaven, thank You for the opportunity to gather here in Your presence.

Bless the people here and guide us. Protect our families and lead us as we lead them."

A unified *"Amen"* ended the prayer and Finley stood up once more.

"Next month is the annual fundraising drive for No Child Goes Hungry. Kathy had organized it every year, but with her recent passing - God rest her soul - it falls on someone else to orchestrate the event. Are there any volunteers?"

A hand shot up in the crowd, followed by another.

"Thank you, Eliza. Thank you, Jake."

The evening went on as people took turns bringing news and events up to attention, making requests and notices aloud for the group to hear as one. Soon, it was my turn to speak.

"As I look around, I see nothing but Sheepdogs."

Murmurs of agreement could be heard among the crowd, along with a lot of head nodding and even a couple of "yeses". 'Sheepdog' is the term given to people who are willing to step up and be leaders of the people who are too afraid, unprepared, or uneducated to act.

"I believe there is a Wolf in our community; I can't prove it, but my gut tells me it's so. I've turned the matter over to the authorities, but if they can't do anything, we might have to. We look out for each other, and we take care of the flock."

Mr. Finley spoke up. "Are you talking about the mean-looking little blonde woman that just moved into town?"

Although this wasn't entirely accurate, I wasn't going to correct him. Niki had rented a little place just outside of a suburb, which to most people was still considered the country. But as far as Old Man Finely was concerned, anything that wasn't out in the sticks was called 'town'.

"Yes, Mr. Finley, I believe that is the same person I was talking about."

"She came to me looking to get a knife repaired. It needed a new handle," Mr. Finely added. "It was an easy fix and she was talking about more knives in her collection needing improvement."

"So, you fixed it for her?" I asked.

"Of course, I did, son. Money's tight these days and hers spends just the same as everyone else's." His tone was defensive.

"I totally understand, and I didn't mean anything by it," I said, trying to quell the situation.

I noticed a few grins and heard a few snickers amongst the other meeting-goers. Everyone knew this was Mr. Finley's normal demeanor, but it still drew a smile.

"I was just trying to get all the facts. Anyways, I think Dave will take care of things as he always does. But I thought it was worth mentioning," I concluded.

The group seemed to agree and understand what I was meaning, and most looked like they were taking mental notes. Even though these people were what some would consider poor and uneducated, they were actually highly intelligent, capable, hard-working, and lived within their means. Just because most - or probably all of them - didn't finish college or live in a big house or drive a new car, other people might have liked to consider them as somehow *less* than the norm, but it simply wasn't true. I loved my group of misfits, and I trusted them with my life.

With no additional business, Mr. Finely closed the meeting and everyone resumed trading. I laid out my pelts and some of the traps I had repaired to re-trade, and looked across the community. You could hear the conversations of exchange, people saying things like *'You're giving me way too much,'* and *'You don't have to do that.'*

Not quite the same thing you would hear at a mall or big box store…

CHAPTER SIX

~John~

The next day, I received a call from Mrs. Collier to report that there was a beaver building a dam in one of their small ponds. People don't realize that beavers can be very destructive on someone's farm, especially when it comes to small, man-made water sources. She said Mr. Collier wasn't feeling well and went to bed right after supper, which isn't like him at all. I told her I'd be right over to take a look and to not worry about it, just take care of the old man.

I had just taken a shower right after work, so I was in my 'old man clothes,' as Em calls them. In other words: jeans, running shoes, and a sweater. I grabbed some clean outdoor clothes, which included my favorite Swedish-made outdoor pants and hoodie, and headed for the garage. On the way, I swung by the kitchen where Maria was on her laptop in the nook. I gave her a kiss and told her where I was going and when I would be back - well, approximately when I would get back. Trapping could consume a lot of time, which sometimes included late nights or even overnighters.

My gear was ready in the garage, so I grabbed my 'go-bag' and headed out. I threw the pack in the seat next to me where it normally rode 'shotgun,' as Em calls the passenger seat.

I made it to the Collier farm with some daylight still left, however I had my headlamp, small flashlight, and fresh batteries for when the great big fireball in the sky went to bed. Even though I didn't make a lot of money, it was evenings like that, spent doing what I love, that made me feel rich.

Mrs. Collier met me in the driveway and explained to me which pond I needed to check, according to her husband. But she also added, "John, he's not been himself lately, so who knows what you'll find - if you find anything at all. He's getting old."

I had to suppress a grin. She didn't know it, but I knew she was a few years older than him.

"Yes, ma'am. Don't you worry yourself about it. I'll take a look around and figure things out," I replied with a warm smile. "Is anyone else on the farm this evening?"

She placed a hand on my cheek. "That's why we love you so much. You're always taking care of everybody else. You're a good man."

I'm sure I blushed, but it was the golden hour, so I hoped she couldn't tell with the warm sun on my face.

"No, nobody else is out here," she continued. "We're not expecting the grandkids until this weekend. It's just us and those pesky beavers."

She turned and slowly made her way up the porch steps, back into the house. I continued to watch for a bit longer, lost in thought about growing old with Maria, and how nice it felt to be sharing this life together with someone so special.

Carrying my happy thoughts from the porch, I made my way to the first pond. When I got there, I didn't notice anything different from before, so I started across the field to the next pond.

I was still lost in blissful thought about family, friends, and life, when I suddenly noticed a movement in the woods.

"Is it a deer? Looks like a deer," I thought out loud.

At the edge of the field, the white tail of a deer waved at me as she ran off in the opposite direction and then quickly disappeared into the forest. My gaze followed her trail and then drifted up into the evening sky, where a red-tailed hawk was riding what I imagined to be a warm current of air.

I hit the jackpot at the next pond. The beavers had been busy. They'd started building a very nice lodge and had quickly begun to destroy the pond. I squatted down to get a better look from ground level. The damage looked worse from that angle, so I got up and made my way to the lodge, circling clockwise.

That's the way I always do a search, clockwise - it helps me remember where I've been.

There it was again...the movement in the woods!

I squatted down again and remained close to the ground for a better look. I sat quiet and still for as long as I could, and then another minute more.

Nothing.

But my gut was telling me there was definitely something out there.

Wait, there it was!

My heightened senses picked up the smell the second it hit my nose. It was the smell of flowers that didn't belong there - the smell of a woman's shampoo.

Then I saw her...the woman in the woods.

I watched Niki walk the edge of the woods, making notes in a small field journal. She hadn't noticed me, and I wasn't planning on letting her. I was only forty yards away, but there was enough space between us to give me plenty of concealment. Still, I wanted to put some more space between us by allowing her to move farther on before I moved again.

With enough expanse to make myself comfortable and give myself room for errors, I slowly stood up to make a move.

When she moved, I moved, mocking her steps and movements. She continued to write and look around.

What was she doing out here? Had the Colliers given her permission to hike or hunt? If Mrs. Collier thought she was okay, then am I missing something? Uh-oh, she stopped while I was still moving, lost in thought.

She looked over her shoulder - *yep, I was busted* - but then she went back to her notebook.

Maybe I was still clear, maybe she didn't hear me.

I continued to stalk her unnoticed for another one hundred yards before Niki stopped again and took off the haversack that was slung over her shoulder. She pulled out a small pad that looked made to sit down on.

With her back to me, it was hard to tell what she was doing. She was going back and forth from her haversack to her notebook. I stood as long as my patience could take it, then silently moved towards her to get a better view.

After about ten yards, I stopped and waited. I started thinking about how I needed to look back to see where I'd been so I wouldn't get turned around, and about what I would do if I needed to move fast away from her.

She seemed focused on her writing, so I slowly turned my head around to take in the path that I had traveled. I was surprised to see that I'd gone a lot farther than I had thought, but then I spotted my path from which I had come. Once I decided I was in good shape, I turned back around to continue surveillance.

But she was gone.

I froze in my tracks and my heart started racing.

Crap! Where did she go?

I controlled my breathing and listened intently. But all I could hear was the *woosh, woosh* of the blood pumping in my ears.

It's hard to focus when your adrenaline is pumping, but that is usually when you need focus most.

Remember, the number one rule is: don't panic.

I slowly took a step in the direction I'd seen her sitting last. Under my feet, I heard a soft c*runch*, then another *crunch*. I stopped to listen. I was as quiet as possible, but the small noise of the leaves under my feet sounded like echoes in the Grand Canyon to me. I got close enough to see where she had been and tried to connect the dots.

Wait...there was something shiny on the ground.

I took another step to get a closer look.

Twang!

The noise of the release was first, then the rushing sound of a swinging limb came from behind and struck me in the back of the leg. I grabbed my backside and arched in pain. I realized then I had sprung a tree spring trap.

This trap was the kind made by bending back a limb and keeping it under tension with a string or cord until the trigger is released. Then, the limb flies back straight to its normal position, striking the one who released the trigger. I fell down to my knees, trying to catch my breath and shake off the hurt.

I looked down and there it was in the dirt - a shiny fishing lure. She had caught a big fish with it, alright. I had never felt more humiliated. Once again, she'd made me feel like an amateur.

"Oh, I'm so sorry. I was practicing my traps and forgot to release this one," a voice said from behind me. "John, are you okay?"

Of course, the voice belonged to Niki. She approached me with her usual brand of expertly feigned concern.

It took everything I had to push through the discomfort and embarrassment before I grabbed the lure off the ground and stood.

"You dropped this," I said as I handed her the lure.

"Don't you want to hold onto it for a keepsake?" She flashed me a smirk and a sly squint of the eyes.

We both stood motionless, looking at each other for what, at the time, seemed like minutes. Though, now I'm sure it was only fifteen or twenty seconds.

She moved first, and it felt like a small victory (at this point, I would've taken anything). She reached out and took the lure from my hand slowly, carefully - like it was liquid.

Then finally, my wits started coming back to me. "What are you doing on this farm?"

"The same as you," she replied quickly.

There it was - she was fishing again, and this time I wasn't going to bite.

I didn't say anything, but I gave her a steely look.

"Scouting, of course. And before you ask, yes, I have permission to be here." Her tone was matter of fact.

That's how I knew she was lying. Finally, I'd caught her up in one. No more suspecting; no more second guessing.

She is a liar.

First of all, I wasn't scouting. I had been called to the farm - invited - which is the only way you get on the Collier farm. Second, Mrs. Collier herself had said that one else was out there. She may have been getting up in age herself, but surely she would have remembered my little blonde 'friend'.

"Well, I better get going. I still have some work to finish," I said, all the while debating whether or not to call her out on her lies.

Maybe if I let her go, I could follow her to see what she'll do next.

Just as it occurred to me that following her hadn't actually worked out so well a little while ago, Niki stepped in close. Before I knew it, she had placed an arm around me and pointed to the pond with the other.

"Is that pond stocked with fish or just for looks?"

What the heck is she doing? We're not friends.

"Look, I've got to go," I said, stepping away. "I'm sure you can find your way back, and don't forget to tell Mrs. Collier you're leaving."

"Ohh. Well, okay then." She suddenly looked puzzled.

She's a good actress - I'll give her that.

The sun was almost behind the horizon and the sky was growing dark. I reached into my pocket and grabbed the small flashlight, turned it on, and shined it back the way I came.

Then she bounded back near to me with a quick step. "Is that the new TruLite LED flashlight?"

"What?" I replied, trying to understand what on earth she was doing. "No, it's a cheap one I got at a flea market. I can't afford expensive gear like that."

"Oh. Well, I thought..."

She allowed her words to trail off and looked down at the ground. Before I knew what had happened, she had placed a palm flat against my chest.

I swatted her hand away and jumped backwards. "Lady, you're crazy!"

She looked around and then, without another word, she slithered off in the opposite direction. I was never so relieved to see someone get out of sight. I couldn't tell where she was going but, honestly, I was just glad she was gone.

I walked a ways back the way I'd come with my flashlight leading the way. When I got to the pond, I looked up and saw Mrs. Collier standing on her back porch, watching me. I waved to her, but she must not have seen me because she never waved back. She just turned and went back inside.

The darned thing was, through all of the commotion, I never did get to do anything about the beavers. I'd have to come back in the morning.

CHAPTER SEVEN

"Ember, it's for you!"

I jumped up from my homework on the porch and ran inside the house. My cell phone didn't get service at home, our being tucked away in the hills, so we were only reachable by landline. I slid into the living room as Mom handed me the phone. I rubbed my neck as I sat down on the couch and placed the receiver to my ear.

"Hello?"

"Hey, girl."

"Oh, hey, Chelsea. What's going on?"

There was a moment of silence on the other end of the line, and that made me a little nervous.

"Chels…?"

Chelsea clucked her tongue and let out a sigh.

"Ember, I overheard something from a friend last period."

"Yeah?"

"I totally played it off, of course, because it's got to be false, but I guess Jada heard the teachers talking about your father and a woman 'rendezvousing' in the woods. Word is, Mrs. Collier saw them."

A feeling of shock came over me.

Now people were talking about Dad and the woman he found in the woods?

"It's false of course, Em, but I felt the need to tell you. You just know how fast word spreads around here, though, about people's affairs."

"'Kay, thanks."

I hung up.

Did she mean "people's affairs" by people's business or people's marital affairs?

I was numb with anxiety as I walked back out to the porch. Mom was reading a gardening magazine, happily unaware of the news. Coming outside, I noticed that a breeze had scattered my papers off of my textbook and across the yard. I slid off the porch and ran after my homework.

So much for doing my schoolwork outside.

As I chased after my papers, fallen leaves scattered about me in the wind, the same way my thoughts were scattering about in my mind. I couldn't focus on any assignment at the moment. Too many other concerns were demanding my attention.

There was Dan, with his troubled eyes and curiosity; I had to know more of his story.

Then there was Frank - *why was he so adamant to know more of what I saw in the forest?*

Finally, these rumors about Dad. I had two options before me: lay low and let others handle whatever the situation was with that Niki-woman or go further sleuthing myself.

I stomped on one paper and grabbed another from the air.

Three more to catch.

Maybe there isn't much to sleuth. Maybe all this has been because I've just been bored with school and home and I want something interesting to happen...

I slowly looked around the yard for the missing papers, knowing good and well that I wouldn't be concentrating on my schoolwork, even if I did manage to catch them.

No, something was going on.

I knew in my gut that my instincts weren't wrong. And I knew that whatever was going on, it had something to do with what happened when we went rushing back to the woods, right before we wrecked.

The loud screech of a hawk broke my train of thought, and turned to see it sitting on an old fence post beside the shed. We didn't have the fence anymore, but the post still stood. I was shocked to see that the hawk was so close.

"I'm looking for my papers. Have you seen them?"

Great, now I'm talking to birds.

The hawk sat perfectly still in its perch, watching me, and then called out once more. I figured that I was alone and it wouldn't hurt to keep talking with the bird.

"The wind carried them away from me and I lost track," I said flippantly.

It cocked its head to the side before it turned and flew into the forest.

Could it be that my papers are in there? Could it be a sign I needed to go back into the forest?

It could have just been that I was crazy and talking to birds.

I started towards the forest, figuring it couldn't hurt to look.

Standing in a place that once felt like home, I now felt the weight of something or someone watching me. I walked out of our clearing into the trees, feeling the brambles reach for me as I passed, hearing the sound of the hawk calling out once more from somewhere in the distance.

'When you're in the woods, something or someone is always watching you; be aware of that.' Dad's words echoed in my head. He'd said it on a hike of ours, years ago, right as I'd started showing interest in these woods. He'd said if it wasn't an animal, it could be another hiker. You never know, but you're never alone.

As I stood there apprehensively at the edge of the tree line, my heart began to pound. Again, I felt the need to return to that spot in the forest to remember what I'd forgotten. Then, I began to sense someone's eyes on me.

"Ember!"

I jumped at the sound of my name being called and skittishly turned around. To my relief, Dad was standing a few yards back, watching me.

"Dinner's done, kiddo. Come on inside, or Mom will have both our hides if we cause it to get cold."

My papers were gone somewhere, carried off into the distance by the wind with no hope of their being found.

Guess I'll have to redo those.

Inside, Mom was putting food on the table. Tanner rushed over to sit as we walked into the room. Dad headed over to wash his hands and I followed, all the while trying to make eye contact with my brother. But he refused to meet my gaze.

"Did you have a good day at school?" Mom's question was for me, but I had one of my own for Tanner.

"Yeah, wasn't too bad. Where've you been Tanner?"

He shrugged, "W-work..."

I knew that was a lie. The brickyard had laid him off and, unless he was still trying his hand at trapping, I doubted he was spending any time in the woods - especially after everything that had happened recently.

Have you ever had a moment full of sounds? Where you're present but only vaguely? One where you hear words spoken in a conversation, but you don't know if it's you or someone else who is saying them?

Somewhere in the back of my mind, I heard the screen door suddenly slam from the back porch. The wind was still rowdy and starting to pick up. My glazed eyes moved as I watched Dad get up close to the door. By instinct, I pulled my sweater tighter around me.

"Getting colder," someone mumbled. *Was it me?*

"Hm?"

Mom finished taking a drink of her water before repeating. "Getting colder out. I'm seeing a lot more of the plants dying. Winter must be coming soon."

I took a stab at my meatloaf as I slowly came out of my trance. "Yeah…"

Dad cleared his throat. "Something on your mind, Ember?"

He eyeballed me, waiting on the answer.

What should I tell him? Where would I start?

I started racking my brain for some way to tell my family that rumors were starting to spread about the blonde lady named Niki, and my dad's visiting her in the forest - that small-town gossip was poisoning the minds of all except the faithful few.

"Just some stuff going around in school. Some teachers talking about you and Niki meeting in the forest. It's kind of weird."

Dad put down his fork and rested his face in his hands, then let out a deep, heavy sigh.

"What they're doing is wrong, and proves that they have nothing better to do with their lives than bring down others... How would they even know we've caught each other in the forest? Sounds like someone else is trespassing on Collier land."

He looked up and met my gaze with a stern glance before returning attention to his food.

"It's best you ignore it and go about your own business, Em," he went on. "All people can do is speculate."

Then it was silent. For a moment, the only noises that disrupted it were the clanking of silverware on plates overtop the wind's beating against the house. Then Tanner finally spoke up.

"Y-you know what? I-it's not r-right though. Aren't you g-going to do s-something? H-how are these r-rumors even g-getting started?" His stammer always got worse as his emotions heightened.

"What we can do" - Dad's tone was calm and matter of fact - "is correct it when someone mentions it to us. *'Vengeance is mine saith the Lord...'*"

...I will repay.

I was annoyed at my father's complacency, so I turned to Mom. "How do you feel about all of this, then? It's as if they're saying- "

"I know what they're saying. I hear it all through the local gossip as well." She rolled her eyes, and a note of annoyance managed to leak through the feigned composure in her tone. "The least they could do is keep their volume down at the store."

Dad shrugged his shoulders. "If it wasn't for the fact she was on Collier land, we wouldn't be crossing paths at all. Now that's enough, y'all, on this topic."

Mom placed her fork on her plate and took a sip of water before clearing her throat. "There's something else going on I've noticed. Have you read today's paper, John?"

Dad shook his head as he continued with his meal.

Mom continued, "There's been more girls gone missing in Wayworth. That's thirty minutes from here. The paper said local authorities were helping with the investigation, but I called Beth at the library and she said that there's been reports in other towns of girls having gone missing. But after a few months the reports lessened... It seems there's a pattern of someone kidnapping these girls and moving on to the next cluster of towns to hit."

I sat in silence as I took in all Mom was saying. Nothing much ever went down in towns like here in Rocky Falls or Wayworth.

"John, what if it's starting here, too? We could be the next town to be hit."

Mom's voice cracked as she finished the thought. Dad took her hand and held it.

"We'll have to be careful, Maria, and keep a closer eye on one another as a family. If they're targeting girls, we'll have to be more guarded about knowing where Ember is at all times."

CHAPTER EIGHT

After dinner, I followed Tanner down to his room. Where mine was chaotic, with its stacked books and messy shelves, Tanner's was calming and organized. His walls were painted a cool blue and he had a few pictures of himself with his friends hung in frames, neatly and in a row. The tops of his dresser and desk were clean and bare, and his shelves had little figurines of animals he'd started carving himself recently. His bed, dressed in a darker shade of blue, was always neatly made.

"Tanner, can we talk?"

He shrugged as he sat down at his desk, picked up his whittling knife, and began working on his newest little figurine. I walked over to his bed and sat on it. It didn't bother him, as long as I smoothed out any wrinkles I made in the cover when I got up.

"Look, I realize something happened in the forest that day you drove me there. I need to know what I saw, or what I found. My phone went missing in the wreck and - "

Tanner slammed his good arm's palm down on the desk and turned at me with eyes full of hurt.

"J-just d-drop it Em! Y-you could g-get in a lot of t-trouble. I'm d-done helping you w-with this..."

He turned back to his work and I stood up. I reckoned I was alone on this, so I headed across the basement into my own room and sat down at my desk with a piece of paper and pen.

I needed to remember what I saw, and I knew I was going to have to make another trip into the forest and back to that spot. The idea of it, though, was enough to make me sick to my stomach. I was losing my nerve after the wreck.

Whatever terrible thing I had found could still be there, and I had the opportunity to finally walk away from it. I could start living my life as if those nasty rumors about Dad weren't being spread all over town, as if the forest was once again a safe place, as if there weren't any dark secrets that needed to be uncovered. That's just it though...they *needed* to be uncovered.

I started thinking about what had gone wrong last time. I didn't remember what happened in the woods, but I did know that if I hadn't lost the phone in the wreck, I would have something to bring back my memories. Apparently, even after searching in the area of the wreck, no one found the phone. It had been as if it'd vanished completely.

What if this time I kept the phone on my person, like in a zipped-up pocket? No, that's not good enough. What if I taped it to my body?

I dropped the pencil and placed my head in my hands. This all felt so ridiculous, and I thought about how irritated I'd be with myself if I were to lose the second phone Dad had given me.

And what if I wrecked all over again and lost my memory...again? What would be the chances of that?

Feeling overwhelmed, I stood and walked over beside my bed, where I'd left my pack. I squatted down next to it, unzipped the pack, and dumped the contents onto the floor. There was my five-by-seven tarp, lightweight blanket, my favorite fixed-blade knife, a metal water container and Billie Cup, a small first aid kit, a hundred feet of paracord, a headlamp, and a pair of wool socks. I slipped on my survival necklace with the ferro-rod and snapped the buckle of my paracord bracelet, attaching it to my wrist. I made sure to add fresh batteries for the headlamp, just like Dad always reminded me: *'You don't want to be caught swallowed up by the dark.'*

I crawled up onto my bed and laid back, then put on my headphones and turned up the music. As the beat reverberated, I could feel it pulsing through me, washing away the anxiety I was starting to feel. My headache was still lingering in the back of my skull. I closed my eyes, hoping to just listen and stop trying to remember. I needed to let go. Closing my eyes, I relaxed and pulled a throw over myself. I was starting to chill, even though my basement bedroom kept consistent temperature throughout the seasons.

Then darkness enveloped me like a frigid cloak.

It's impenetrable,
this new darkness, such
that I can't tell where the
sky and ground collide.
There is a total absence
of stars - I can't even see

my hands. It is totally silent. It almost feels as if I've found myself at the bottom of some type of abyss. I realize my arms are wrapped around my front, and my knees are pulled tight to my chest. I release myself and stretch out to lay back. I'm so tired... I rest my head on the ground and realize there's something uneven beneath it.

I shoot up to turn around to feel for whatever it could have been. I'm using my sense of touch to see. I feel loose soil under my fingers. I try to flatten it, but as it gives away and I feel it become replaced by some sort of fabric. I pull on it, and feel something heavier come up with it. I move my fingers down the object and realize it has a familiar feel to it. I feel further up the object, letting my fingers see as much as they can, right up until my fingers interlock with its fingers.

Lightning strikes with an extremely loud roar of thunder, and light emanates through the sky. For that one fleeting moment, I see that I'm lying on dirt and surrounded by tall, bare trees that reach high up

I woke up with a chill running down my spine and sweat pouring from my face. Mom was standing above me, putting a damp cloth on my head.

"I came down and found you shivering with a fever, honey. Why don't I get you some medicine- "

I pushed her hand away and my voice cracked as I spoke.

"I remember, Mom. I remember everything..."

Tears started pouring down my face as Mom pulled me into a hug.

"Oh, Em, it's going to be alright. What did you see, sweetie?"

I pulled out of the hug and rubbed my eyes with my arm.

"Go get Dad, Mom. Please, I need to talk to him. Something really bad is being hidden in the forest."

Dad was working in the garage when Mom found him and told him. He rushed down to my room and found me sitting on my bed, staring down at the floor with my knees pulled up into my chest and my arms wrapped around myself. The entire scene in the forest was as clear as day now - everything I was rushing to tell Dad before the wreck.

"Dad..."

He sat down on my bed beside me and pulled me into his chest.

"It's okay, Em. Just take it slow."

I started out with where I had been.

"Dad, do you remember where we were when I saw that woman burying something?"

"Yeah, I do."

"I went back there, but from the direction of the forestry road. It started storming as I was digging, and what I found buried was... a handkerchief."

Dad seemed to be thinking as his eyebrows furrowed.

"What color was it?"

"It was red. That's not all, though..."

"I remember seeing a red scarf on someone recently, actually. What else did you see, Em?"

My heart was beating so hard; I could still see it, rising from the earth as I pulled up the bright red cloth.

"Dad, the scarf was tied to a human hand."

CHAPTER NINE

~Ember~

I stood there waiting with no sign of Mom or Dad. Tanner didn't mention picking me up late. I slid down the wall and collapsed onto the ground, letting out a sigh. They'd never been this late before; I should've just taken the bus.

Maybe they left me a text or missed call.

I rummaged around in my pack, only to find a dead phone and the realization that I had left the charger at home.

Well, that stinks.

The front parking lot of the school was completely empty. The only noise was the highway in the distance. I got out my journal and tried sketching the school itself, but I was close to losing my mind from wondering where my parents were.

I looked at the clock through the window to the foyer entrance: 4:30.

Maybe I should call them from inside the school.

The doors remained locked to the outside at all times, so I looked inside for signs of anyone. My face pressed against the glass, waiting…

There!

Two people were walking from the hallway into the lobby; one was pushing a broom and the other, a trash can. Recognizing one of the janitors to be Mr. Frank, I started banging on the doors with my fists.

Mr. Frank ran over and pushed the door open.

"Hey, girl, what're you still doing here?"

I shrugged my pack onto my shoulder and headed in.

"Well, no one's here to get me so I feel that I should call someone. Kind of frustrated, but things happen I guess."

"Yeah? I'm sorry about that. Hey, this is the new guy Max. Showin' him the ropes of pushing a broom around. I'll be a minute to put stuff up, then I can take ya home if you want."

"Nah, it's fine. I just gotta find a phone to call my parents."

But Mr. Frank was already hurrying both Max and the broom down the hallway towards the janitor's closet.

"No, really! It's fine."

Well, I don't want to make him go out of his way. I barely know the guy, anyhow...

I decided to turn around and go the other direction.

I walked down the hall pulling on doors, and found each classroom and office to be locked. No one else seemed to be there, or, if they were, they didn't seem to notice me. I remembered that Mr. Frank had keys on his belt, and I felt safe to assume that if each one went to a door, sure one of those doors could be an office with a phone.

Or better yet, why didn't I ask to use his phone?

I turned back around to look for the janitors and found Max just around the corner, walking alone down the hallway. He was tall and lanky, with mussed blonde hair and boyish eyes. For all I knew, he might've recently graduated.

"Hey, where's Frank?"

Max shrugged. "He's in one of the offices, not sure which one, said he had to do something real fast. My phone's in my car or else I'd let you use it. Maybe Frank will let you use an office phone."

"Yeah, maybe. Thanks, anyways. It was nice to meet you."

"Nice to meet you, too."

As I walked past him and further down the hallway, I realized Mr. Frank never gave him my name.

"I'm Ember, by the way!"

But when I looked, Max was gone.

From somewhere close, I heard the sounds of a door's slamming shut and a set of keys shaking together, so I set off to follow them. Finally, I found Mr. Frank and ran up to him.

"Hey, did that office have a phone? If so, could you let me back in there to make a call? Or could I use your phone?"

"I called your dad for you. He said he's running behind and he doesn't mind if I drop you off."

A feeling of annoyance overcame me, and my face clearly showed it, but another feeling creeped into the back of my mind: *doubt.*

"Really? That's annoying. I wish he would've sent someone by now."

"Like you said, things happen. C'mon kiddo."

Something else came to my mind. "Did he mention what land he was calling from? Billinger's or Danny's?"

I watched his face intently, waiting for his answer.

What would he say?

Mr. Frank shrugged.

"Sounded like Danny. Is he an uncle or friend of yours?"

Neither. He doesn't exist.

"Eh, a friend, I suppose. Hey, can I use the restroom really fast?"

We were walking pretty quickly now, and Mr. Frank kind of seemed in a hurry.

"I guess. Hurry up."

Now he was getting short with me. He was never short with me.

I dashed to the bathroom and looked around.

Bad idea, no windows. Why didn't I think about that? Ok, think fast. What options do I have? What can I do?

Hearing footsteps, I gripped my pack tightly and ducked into a stall.

He neared the entrance of the bathroom and called in. "Hurry now, I've got places to be."

Oh man, oh man, oh man!

My hands started shaking, and I took note that I couldn't show my nerves or else he'd know I figured something was up.

"Will do!"

This isn't all in my head - this can't be. I wish it was. It would be easier if it was. Why didn't I stay outside and just wait? Where is Mom or Dad?

I flushed the toilet and proceeded onward to wash my hands. This time, I mindfully put my pack only on one shoulder. When I stepped out of the bathroom, I saw him cease what looked to have been incredibly impatient pacing.

"Sorry, I'm good now."

We started walking towards an exit - *a side exit,* I noted. I was still noticeably shaking.

"Do you think it's cold in here? I should get my sweater out of my pack."

"Nah, we're almost outside."

He opened the door and placed his hand on my shoulder.

"But it's cool outside, too."

The only vehicle in the parking lot was a red truck with dark tinted windows. I wished it was Dad's.

Mr. Frank was walking faster now - we were almost jogging - and his hand starting to grip my shoulder. In a sudden desperation, I found my nerve and jerked away from him. He grabbed my pack and I slipped out of it as I tried to sprint off.

I heard him right on my heels, breathing heavily as he chased me.

I wasn't fast enough.

He grabbed me from behind and picked me up, then tossed me head-first over his shoulder with my back against his.

A scream left my mouth as the sky rose to meet the ground. The blood rushed to my face, and the panic dropped from my chest and into my throat.

"Please- "

When we made it to the truck and he dropped me off of his shoulder, the world blurred back into its former position. And as I fell to the ground like a bag of trash, I felt all hope of seeing parents leave my heart.

After separating me from my pack, he tossed it into the bed of the truck and shoved me into the cab. Then he grabbed a gun out of the glove compartment, slammed my door shut, and walked around to the other side of the truck. I tried opening my door, but the child lock must've been on.

CHAPTER TEN

~John~

I pulled into the driveway and opened the gate. Once I'd driven through, I had to stop and get out to close the gate back. It was a little extra work and sometimes annoying, but it provided an extra layer of security. The real security, however, wasn't in the gate itself, but in the motion-sensor on the gate that would alert anyone in the house that the gate had been opened or closed.

I could see Maria as I made my way the drive. She was standing on the porch with her arms folded across her chest, and she wore a distinct frown on her face.

"Uh oh, something isn't right," I muttered to myself.

I put Nelly in park and then hesitated, knowing something was wrong. I stayed seated a moment and looked around, first right, then left. Maria was still standing in the same position on the porch. I decided to get out of the truck. As I did, I reached under the seat and grabbed my small pistol (I had a concealed carry license to legally carry it or keep it in my vehicle). I placed it in the waistline of the back of my pants and walked towards her.

"Hello, Maria. How are you?" This wasn't a normal greeting, by any stretch - it was code for 'I know something is wrong'.

She got right to the point; no beating around the bush for her.

"I got a call from Mrs. Collier!" she said, tapping her foot. (Yep, just like in the old cartoons when the mom would get mad at the cat for misbehaving.) "What were you doing out there with that woman?"

So that's what this is about.

Inside relief washed through me, which Maria sensed immediately. She didn't like that any better.

"I'm serious, John. What were you doing with that young woman!" She came off the porch and lunged at me. This time, it was more of a statement than a question.

"What? You can't be serious?" I said on the defensive.

Now she was in front of me. She raised a finger and pointed in my face. "If you think I'm going to allow you to cheat on me- "

"Whoa, whoa... That's enough!" I cut her off. "Whatever happened to innocent until proven guilty?"

She lowered the finger that was pointed in my face.

"You know me better than that. Where did you get this from?"

"Well...I'd rather not say." Her eyes filled with tears, then the anger reappeared in her voice. "But it's a pretty reliable source, and you already know that even Ember has heard some things from friends at school. And then today, I got a call asking if you had a partner now - a partner who stays really close to you!" She let that simmer. "You know...a pretty blonde lady from out of town!" she said, as her voice grew louder.

Oh, the troubles of a small town.

She was looking in my eyes with fire in her own, and I gently placed my hands on her shoulders.

"Honey the last thing I want in my life is another female."

She gave a slight laugh, then smacked my chest with a free hand. "Jerk!"

She feigned resistance as I drew her in close and said, "You know I love you more than anything in the world - you and the kids

119

are my world. I wouldn't do anything to jeopardize that. Besides, I love you and I'm still in love with you. Nothing could change that."

"Then what is going on? What's happening to our little family?" She laid her head on my chest.

As we climbed the front porch steps and entered the house, I said, "I'm not sure, but we will find out together."

I felt better knowing we were momentarily back on the same team.

"Now, where's Ember?" I asked. "Let's find out what she's heard and put this thing to rest."

The shock hit her like a gut punch.

"John, I thought you were picking her up. I was so mad I didn't even realize she wasn't with you." She placed a hand on her cheek. Her eyes filled with tears again, and her neck and ears grew red as she looked out the front door at my truck.

"Didn't Tanner pick her up?" I felt my own face burn as my blood began to rush in panic.

Right on que, Tanner came out of the kitchen and into the living room, munching on an apple.

"Hey, Dad." he said through a mouthful of fruit as he plopped down on the couch.

"*John! No!*" Maria cried out. "Where's Em? Who's got Ember?"

Now she had both hands wrapped up in my shirt. I had to remind myself of the number one rule: *Don't Panic.*

I reached into my pocket for my phone, pulled it out, and called Ember. Maria watched wide-eyed.

It went to voicemail after two rings. "Em, it's Dad. Call me when you get this, kiddo."

I tried to remain calm for two reasons: one, for Maria, and two, for Ember, so she wouldn't think something was wrong when she got the message.

Maria, clearly shaken, seated herself on the edge of the couch next to Tanner, who, at this point, had stopped eating.

"D-did I do something wrong? Was I supposed to get Ember?"

"No, buddy, it's not your fault. Clearly it is a mix up on all our parts, but nobody's to blame."

I looked at Maria. She was still in shock, staring blankly at the floor with a glazed look over her face.

Then suddenly, like being awakened from a dream, she snapped her head up at me. "I know what's happening. I know what Niki in the woods is doing." She slowly came to her feet.

"She's stealing girls," she said quietly. "She's part of the human trafficking happening in nearby towns. I just feel it in my gut."

It was as if time had stopped.

"John, she's taken our daughter." Her voice grew louder. She was half-shouting and half-crying. *"John, she's got our Ember!"*

Now, I was the one in shock. I felt the horror of what could be happening. I had to calm myself and Maria down.

I took a second to say a quick prayer to myself. *"Oh Lord my God please don't let this be true."*

I looked back up at my family. "Let's calm down… I will drive to the school and pick her up if she's still there. Maria, you start calling her friends to see if anyone knows her whereabouts. Tanner, you do the same - after all she is in high school now and some of her friends do drive. She may have gotten a ride home."

Maria wasn't buying it, but she at least was on her phone, doing something.

Tanner placed his apple on the side table and started dialing. He had lots of friends, and even though he was the definition of an introvert, he was a very popular guy. Everyone loved him, but what was not to love?

I did an about-face and headed back out the door.

"I've got my phone. Call me when you find her. I'll turn around and come back home." I spoke with confidence. But it was only a show. Once outside, I raced to the truck fearing the worst had already happened.

CHAPTER ELEVEN

I woke up on a cold concrete floor. When I rolled over to look around, my head felt groggy and I started to cough.

Have I been drugged?

It was dark. But there was a bit of light coming through the thin blankets that covered the small windows near the ceiling, and it was enough for me to assess my surroundings. I could tell that I was in some sort of a basement. The walls were also concrete, lined with rows of empty shelves. I could make out two doors with poor paint jobs, and I didn't know which one led upstairs, or where the other one even led to. There was a chain hanging from a naked, unlit bulb in the middle of the room that seemed to be the only light source other than the windows.

I started panicking. But I wasn't tied up, and I wasn't restrained. That confused me the most. Apparently, I didn't pose a threat of escaping to Mr. Frank.

All of a sudden, I heard a *thump, thump, thump* moving towards me.

Someone's coming!

I could hear that the footsteps were coming down a set of stairs, so I rolled back over and closed my eyes. The person opened the door. I wanted to hold my breath, to hide. I could feel someone's gaze on me, searching for any signs of change.

Is it Mr. Frank? Could someone else be here? Do I breathe as if I'm still asleep?

My heart was in my throat. I still don't know how long they stood there - it felt like forever. But even once the door finally, quietly clicked closed, I continued to stay still. After counting to sixty a dozen times, I allowed myself to slowly open my eyes and roll over again.

I was relieved to find myself all alone, but now I had to figure out how I was going to get out. I stood up, my head still fuzzy. I couldn't risk going through either door, so the windows were my only resolve. And with that, it was time to go.

First, I ran over to the door and pressed my ear against the door.

Nothing.

Then, I ran over to one of the windows. It was high up, but if I jumped, I could grab onto it with my hands and hoist myself up. I'd have to break the glass first, though...*and what if someone hears me?* I needed to act fast and to be as quiet as possible.

I looked around again to try and find anything that could help me, but there was nothing on the floor and nothing on the shelves. I stood there alone, feeling cold inside with fear and desperation, and my eyes began to well at the thought of what might come next.

I took a deep breath. There was no time to waste.

I removed my sweater and my shirt, then put my sweater back on and zipped it closed.

"God, please help me…"

It was a small basement window, about two feet long by one foot tall. I jumped and grabbed onto the windowsill, but then slipped and fell to the floor. Holding my breath, I listened for footsteps.

Nothing.

I got up quickly and tried again, and this time I was able to hold on long enough to pull myself up to the window.

It was a small space to crawl through and an even smaller ledge onto which I'd have to hold my perch - I wouldn't be able to use my foot to smash it from here. Thankfully, the pane looked relatively thinner than most windows, as if it were older and possibly original with the house. Carefully, so as to not fall off, I took my shirt and wrapped it around my hand as best as I could, hoping to protect it.

Then, with all the force I had mustered up, I reared my arm back and punched through the glass. The window smashed with a shattering sound – much louder than I would have liked. My shirt hadn't been thick enough to fully protect my hand, which was now throbbing from the severe stabbing of the shards. But there was no time to stop.

I got as much of the glass out of the pane as I could before crawling through, all the while looking for any sign of my captor - or anyone else for that matter. As far as I could tell, the coast was clear.

Holding my bloodied hand to my chest, I darted to the back of the shed. My goal was to run directly into the woods and not stop. Then, I saw what I was pretty sure was my pack, nestled into the outdoor trash can. The can's lid was raised from being overfilled, and the strap was peeking out from underneath a bag of trash. I grabbed it, stuffed my shirt down into it, and turned to face the tree line where the forest met the yard. Once more, with sweat beading on my forehead, I held my breath.

For a moment, I stared at the tree line. I thought about what was lying behind it. How cruel it seemed now - cruel and riddled with buried secrets. I had no way of knowing if I would make it out safely, but the forest was calling to me, offering asylum.

With no other option before me, I ran.

* * *

Excerpt From Book Three

The wind whipped my hair loose as I raced down the hill. I was somewhere between falling and running, holding nothing back, gaining more and more speed. All that mattered was putting distance between myself and the eyes that I'd felt in the basement made of concrete. I saw the trees streaking past in my peripheral vision as a woman's voice suddenly rang out from somewhere behind me.

"Where you going to go? I'll find you! Can't run for long!"

The voice belonged to Niki.

I know what she's a part of. I know what this boils down to: life or death.

My calves were burning, and my chest hurt as the cold air stung inside my lungs. Taking no time to strategically cross, I splashed through the creek and took the path of least resistance between two other banks.

Time to start thinking.

I can't outrun her for long. I can't go the way I came. She's hunting me. I'm the animal. Don't break branches. Don't step on twigs.

Just then I realized that the branches, the twigs, the trees around me were all familiar. I knew this part of the forest.

Spider web ahead - duck!

My chest was all but killing me now, and my abdomen was burning. But I knew what I was looking for. I just had to go a bit further now...

There!

I sprinted up to the base of a hill, utop of which lived two trees that shared a base - my 'Twin Trees'. I started scurrying up and around the side of the hill, taking switchbacks to conserve energy. I grabbed onto trees to pull myself up faster as I pounded my way upward, moving somewhere between a hike and run.

I knew I couldn't stray from listening to her for even a second, and I heard her movements echoing through the trees behind me.

She's not far behind. She might even be crossing the creek now.

The hill was more like a mountain, living on the edge of the landscape's transition into higher and higher altitudes. After a grueling climb, I finally reached the top, an area filled with boulders and a lookout with a steep drop off.

There, securely anchored and hidden between two particular boulders, was a commando rope bridge Dad had made years ago. One of the two ropes was tied to the trees on either side, and the other was staked into the ground, stretching out across the ravine.

I climbed over the boulders. I was perfectly hidden for now, and hopefully that would buy me time. Stepping onto the lowest rope while holding onto the top one, I started swaying. The wind picked up, and the sky showed signs of a storm.

Moving quickly but surely, I tried to stay as steady as possible without rocking the bridge too much. This rope bridge had visibly been up for a while - it was the start of what Dad called the Appalachian highway and was showing signs of weathering.

I looked over my shoulders and saw my assailant, Niki, who was just now reaching the top. I turned around, moving faster.

I had almost made it to the end of the bridge when I felt it shake, suddenly and violently. I looked over my shoulder and saw her moving quickly behind me.

When I reached the other side, it was time to act quickly - she was coming closer. I fished my knife from my pocket and started sawing at the top rope, hard and fast. The rope gave way and flew past me, and I heard her let out a curse.

She fell forward and grabbed the second rope, then started shimmying her way across with both her legs and arms. But I was already working diligently on the second and lowest rope. She was approaching faster and had almost reached the ledge when it suddenly gave way.

I heard her scream as she disappeared into the ravine.

I looked down to see if my assailant had fallen and found her dangling, still holding on tightly to the rope with her right hand. Her left arm had gone limp.

The clouds roared with thunder as lightning lit up the sky. I ran deeper into the forest. I had to get off the top of the hills, fast.

The storm was here.

Rain was pouring, hard and loud. I raced downward, heading deeper into unfamiliar territory.

Would she come after me still?

It would take a while. I couldn't run all night in this storm, and I couldn't get my bearings out in the middle of it. I had to find shelter and hide for the night.

"Oof!" My shoe caught on something.

As I fell, I tucked in my shoulder and rolled, but I couldn't stop myself and quickly began to pick up speed. I tried to slow myself by unfolding my body, but ended up tumble-flailing downward until, suddenly, my back smacked right into the trunk of a tree.

"Aaaah...!"

I tried to muffle my groaning. A sharp pain seared into the lower-right side of my back and shot upward into my torso. I reached backwards to feel it, and the twisting of my muscles sharpened the stabbing feeling that was already there. I felt around in my rain-soaked jacked for the center of the pain and realized that it had become soaked with something else - something warm and thick and sticky.

No time to lose. Pick yourself up and find shelter.

I used the tree as support and slowly stood up. My trail was too obvious. I had to hide the blood so she wouldn't know I was injured. The rain was still coming down, heavy and hard.

Could it wash away my trail? What about my shelter? Dad, I need you! I don't know what to do. I'm scared.

I was finally back by, what I thought may be, the same creek I had crossed before. But it was larger now, and I couldn't be sure. Thunder sounded and lightning struck somewhere close-by. Now that I was in the lowest point of the area I'd encountered so far, I had to find a thicket of trees or shrubs.

The trees seemed to grow thicker on the other side of the creek, but it was getting darker, and I couldn't tell for certain. My back was throbbing now, and my feet were killing me - my hiking boots weren't good for running. I needed rest.

I jogged as best I could alongside the creek until I came to a shallower part. I quickly splashed through the rushing waters and held my pack high above my head. The rocks were slippery, and my foot went out from under me, but I caught myself before I fell. Still, when I did, even more pain shot up through my back.

The sun was almost fully set, and with it, my pace slowed to a walk. I crossed another hill, another puddle of water. My breathing turned into wheezing. The feelings of panic, doubt, and fear crept into my thoughts to accompany my already feeling like a hunted animal.

It had become surreally dark. It was the kind of darkness that coexisted with impossible silence. I stopped to listen, longing to hear the slightest sound or notion of existence, whether it be human or animal, but I heard nothing. I couldn't tell what would have been scarier: the idea that something was following me, or the idea that I was completely alone.

Thankfully, the moon shone bright, and I could tell that I was finally in the thick of the trees. I made my way carefully and quickly, fully aware of my movements, so as to leave little in the wake of my path.

A large fir tree, with heavy branches that drooped and rested low to the ground, began to beckon to me. I crawled underneath it and rested my side against its trunk. A new rush of panic came over me again as I noticed the zipper of my pack had come partially open and that some of my gear had gone missing. The brown tarp at the bottom was still folded and safe, but my matches, my compass, and my first aid kit were all gone. At least I still had the fixed-blade knife, folding hand saw, folding shovel, and my shirt in the pack.

The storm was finally dying down. Exhausted, I cut some pine boughs from the tree and gathered some of the fallen needles and made a bed to lay on - this would create a barrier between myself and the cold ground. I pulled out my tarp, wrapped myself in it, and laid down using my pack as a pillow. I curled myself around the trunk of the tree - it was something strong to hold onto, something steady and constant.

Sleep overcame me as the creek swelled over the banks.